This book belongs to

Princess _____

The Royal Disney Princess Club

Every Disney Princess Adores Dancing

Dance

Story adaptation by Thea Feldman. Crafts and activities by Kris Hirschmann.

Photography by White Light Incorporated, Bethel, CT

Design by Mark A. Neston Design

Published by Scholastic Inc., 90 Old Sherman Turnpike, Danbury, CT 06816.

For information regarding permission, write to: Disney Licensed Publishing, 114 Fifth Ave., New York, NY 10011.

ISBN-13: 978-0-545-08518-2   ISBN-10: 0-545-08518-7
U.K. ISBN-13: 978-0-545-08557-1   U.K. ISBN-10: 0-545-08557-8

Printed in Singapore

First printing, October 2008

Cinderella
Dancing Dreams

A Storybook with Crafts & Activities

O ne sunny afternoon, Cinderella tended to the laundry while her stepmother, Lady Tremaine, and her stepsisters, Anastasia and Drizella, had tea. All Cinderella's stepsisters could talk about was the grand ball they would attend that evening.

"This will be our third one this month!" bragged Anastasia.

"Everyone is sure to envy our new gowns!" Drizella added.

"Perhaps you will both find husbands at last," sniffed Lady Tremaine, as she sipped her tea.

Cinderella sighed. How she wished she could attend a ball! Cinderella couldn't think of anything more wonderful than to dress up in a beautiful gown, ride in a carriage, and dance the night away with a handsome gentleman.

She turned to her dog, Bruno, who was dozing lazily by the laundry basket. "I wish I could go, too," she whispered to him, "just this once." But Cinderella knew that her cruel stepmother would never allow it.

Later that evening, Cinderella's stepmother and stepsisters went off to the ball, without so much as a glance in Cinderella's direction. "Left behind again," Cinderella remarked to no one in particular. She wasn't surprised at all. Because even when her stepfamily didn't have a party or a ball to attend, they ignored Cinderella—unless, of course, they were barking orders at her.

Instead of feeling sorry for herself, though, Cinderella decided to get started on the next day's chores. While she dusted behind an old chest, a small hidden drawer popped open! Inside was a beautiful pink hair band. "How pretty!" Cinderella said. "I don't think it would do any harm if I tried it on."

Back in her room, Cinderella showed the hair band to her little friends Jaq and Gus. "Put it on, Cinderelly, put it on!" Jaq urged, as he and Gus jumped up in front of the mirror.

"All right!" said Cinderella with a smile. She carefully placed the band in her hair. "Well, how do I look?" she asked her friends.

Jaq and Gus just stared back at her.

Then Cinderella looked at her reflection in the mirror and gasped. She was dressed in a beautiful ball gown fit for a princess! At first, Cinderella couldn't believe her eyes.

But Jaq was smiling from ear to ear and Gus was jumping up and down. They saw it, too!

Delightedly, Cinderella lifted the folds of her skirt and began to dance and twirl around the room.

"Bruno *has* to see this!" shouted Cinderella. She took off
the hair band and rushed to rouse the dog from his latest nap.
Cinderella brought Bruno back to her room. "Now watch me,
Bruno," Cinderella said, while she again put on the hair band.

Magically, Cinderella was once again dressed for a fancy ball. To her surprise, Cinderella saw that Bruno had disappeared and a distinguished gentleman with a cane stood in his place!

"Bruno?" Cinderella asked in disbelief.

Bruno nodded and then bowed to Cinderella, as if inviting her to dance.

"Why, I would be delighted," she said with a laugh.

Arm in arm, she and Bruno waltzed and whirled and twirled around the room for hours. It wasn't until they heard the *clip-clop* of the horse-drawn carriage bringing her stepfamily home that their dancing came to an end.

Reluctantly, Cinderella took off the magical hair band, and instantly she and Bruno became their ordinary selves once more.

The next day, Cinderella went about her chores with a lighter heart than usual. When Bruno approached her while she was feeding the chickens, Cinderella had to smile. "Good morning, sir," she said, as she curtsied.

Anastasia and Drizella called for Cinderella to bring them their breakfast, only to find her dancing her way down the hall.

"What *are* you doing?" shrieked Anastasia.

"And what do you have to be so happy about?" sneered Drizella.

But Cinderella paid no attention to them. "I'll be back with your breakfast soon," she sang.

Later that night, long after her stepfamily had retired for the evening, Cinderella tiptoed out of the house with Bruno and her mice friends close behind. "We *must* share the magic with Major," she said softly, as they walked toward the barn.

Inside, Cinderella showed the hair band to her horse, Major. Then she placed the band on her head and closed her eyes, hoping the magic would work again.

The hair band twinkled and sparkled as Cinderella looked down to find herself dressed once more in the lovely pink gown. And not only was Bruno there beside her, with his cane in hand; but Major had become a handsome gentleman as well, dressed in fine clothing.

"This is beginning to feel like a real ball," said Cinderella happily. "Now I have not one but *two* dance partners!"

Bruno and Major smiled back at their friend, more than happy to take turns dancing with her.

As she danced around the barn, Cinderella couldn't remember the last time she had been so happy. Delightful music filled the air. The haystacks and horse stalls had turned into fancy curtains and stately columns. The barn had become a ballroom! And Jaq, Gus, and the rest of her mice friends were there. All of them had been transformed into guests at the ball!

"Well, how do you do?" Cinderella called out joyously to her friends, while they all began to dance around her.

The festivities went on until the wee hours of the morning. It was only when the sun began to rise and the rooster called out his morning greeting that the dancing finally had to come to an end.

The magical dance was the closest thing to a ball Cinderella had ever experienced. It was a night she would always remember.

Later that day, Cinderella was thinking of the magical dance when she heard a knock at the front door. She hurried downstairs to find that an invitation to a royal ball had just been delivered.

"By royal command, every eligible maiden is to attend," her stepmother read aloud.

Maybe this time, Cinderella's wicked stepmother would allow her to attend a real ball! "Anything is possible," Cinderella thought to herself, "now that I know dreams can come true."

The End

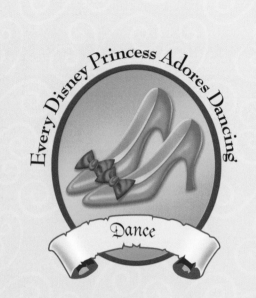

Every Disney Princess Adores Dancing

Dance

This month's princess theme is dance.

These crafts and activities will show you different ways
to enjoy dancing.

Cinderella's Crafts & Activities

When Cinderella discovers a magical hair band, her dreams of dancing at a fancy ball come true! Turn the page to discover Cinderella's crafts and activities about dancing.

Ballerina Princess

You will dance with joy every day when you display this adorable ballerina princess in your room!

What You Need

- Paintbrush
- Paint (any color)
- Round-headed wooden clothespin (available at craft stores)
- Permanent markers
- 3-inch (7.5-cm) circle of see-through fabric (any color)
- Scissors
- White glue
- 4-inch (10-cm)-long pink, tan, or brown chenille stem (pipe cleaner)
- Glitter glue, stick-on jewels, and other items

With a grown-up's help:

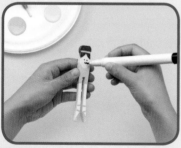

1. Paint the ballerina's face and legs and let dry. Paint the ballerina's hair and let dry. Paint the hair band, leotard, and toe shoes and let dry. Draw the ballerina's facial features with the markers as shown.

2. Fold the fabric circle in half and then in half again. Cut off about ¼ inch (6 mm) of the point as shown to make a small hole in the center.

3. Cut a slit from one side of the outer circle into the small inner circle.

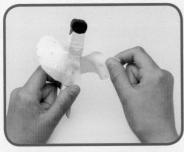
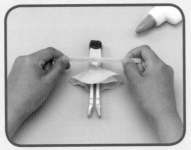
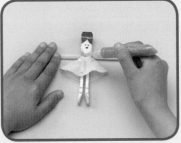

4. Spread a line of glue around the ballerina's "waist" (just above where the wooden legs separate). Starting at the back of the clothespin, press the inside open end of the fabric circle against the glue, wrapping the fabric around her waist. Hold in place until dry.

5. Place the ballerina facedown on a flat surface. Squeeze a blob of glue on her back, just above the skirt where shown. Lay the chenille stem across the ballerina's back, making sure it is centered. Press the stem into the glue. Let the glue dry completely.

6. Decorate your ballerina with glitter glue, stick-on jewels, or anything else you like to give her a special princess sparkle.

Stage a Ballet

Create an entire company of ballerinas. Design a different costume for each dancer or make matching wardrobes. It's up to you! When you are done, set up a little stage and play some ballet music. Use your ballerinas as puppets to act out an entire ballet for your friends and family.

Magical Hair Band

Cinderella becomes the belle of the ball when she puts on her magical hair band. You will want to dance the night away, too, when you wear this sparkly accessory that you make yourself!

- 18-inch (46-cm)-long piece of pink cloth ribbon, 1½ inches (3.8 cm) wide
- Glue stick
- 36-inch (91-cm)-long piece of sparkly silver cloth ribbon, ¼ inch (6 mm) wide
- Scissors
- Glitter, fabric paint, sequins, stick-on jewels, and other items to decorate your hair band

With a grown-up's help:

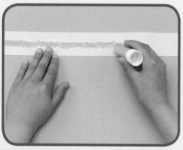

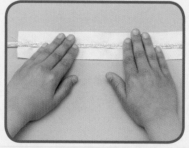

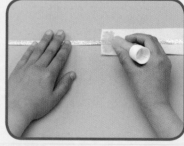

1. Lay the pink ribbon on a flat surface. Spread a line of glue along the center of the ribbon as shown.

2. Gently lay the silver ribbon along the strip of glue. Adjust the ribbons so that an equal amount of silver ribbon extends on either side of the pink ribbon, then press the ribbons together.

3. Spread glue along the last 1½ inches (3.8 cm) of both ends of the pink ribbon along both sides of the silver ribbon as shown.

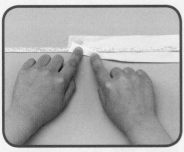

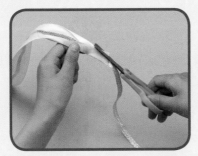

4. Fold up the bottom edge as shown of both ends of the pink ribbon and press in place.

5. Repeat for the top edge of both ends of the pink ribbon. Cut off the overlapping points of the pink ribbon.

6. Turn over the hair band. Decorate your brand-new hair band with glitter, fabric paint, sequins, stick-on jewels, or anything else you like.

Royal Idea

When the glue and paint are completely dry, lay the hair band across your head. Tuck the band behind your ears to hold your hair out of your face. Then lift your hair and ask a grown-up or a friend to tie the silver ends against your neck. You are ready to dance, just like Cinderella!

Princess Pizzazz

Do you have lots of plain hair bands around your room? If so, try spicing them up with a little princess pizzazz! Stick-on jewels, glitter, sparkly ribbons, sequins, and other special details will give your old hair bands a whole new look. You will look and feel like royalty when you wear these lovely headpieces!

No-Sew Dancing Skirt

Cinderella feels as pretty as a princess when she dances in her long, flowing skirt. It's easy to make your own dancing skirt.

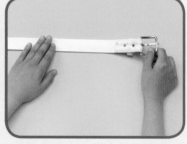

What You Need

- 1 yard (.91 m) of 60-inch (1.5-m)-wide fabric (any color)
- Scissors
- No-longer-needed child-sized belt

With a grown-up's help:

1. Cut the fabric in half so that you have two 30- x 36-inch (76- x 91-cm) pieces of fabric.

2. Lay one of the pieces on a table with the 36-inch (91-cm)-long edges on the top and bottom. Cut the fabric into strips about 3 inches (7.5 cm) wide and 30 inches (76 cm) long. Repeat to cut the other piece of fabric into strips.

3. Lay the belt facedown on a flat surface.

Crafts & Activities

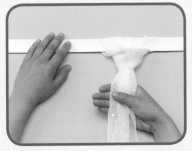

4. Fold one fabric strip in half. Poke the folded end under the belt as shown.

5. Bend the two ends of the fabric down, over the belt, and poke them through the loop in the strip. Pull gently until the loop is snugly knotted against the belt.

6. Working outward from the middle, repeat steps 4 and 5 to attach the rest of the fabric strips to the belt, making sure each loop is looped next to the previous one.

♡ Royal Idea

Ask a grown up to help you put on your skirt with the buckle in the back. Look in the mirror to see your show-stopping creation! Like the ballerina, you are ready for the dance!

Royal Ball

Cinderella longs to be invited to a royal ball. It takes a long time for her special moment to arrive. You and your friends, however, don't have to wait another minute. You can dance, dance, dance at a princess-perfect party you throw yourselves!

Choose a Place

Your very first step is to choose the best location for your party. A big family room, a large porch, or even a clean garage would be perfect places.

Clear the Dance Floor

Decide exactly where you want people to dance, then mark off the area. You might use an old carpet as your dance floor, or with a grown-up's help, you might outline a dance area with masking tape.

Gather Your Audience

Cinderella loves to dance with her animal friends, so remember to include your animal friends in the fun, too! Gather your favorite stuffed pals and scatter them all over your dancing room.

Plan Your Menu

Dancing is hard work! Your princess party pals are sure to get hungry and thirsty during your party. Offer pink lemonade, finger sandwiches, and other dainty treats to fill your friends' royal tummies.

Crafts & Activities

Select Your CDs

You can't have a royal ball without your favorite music! Decide in advance what music you want to play. To keep things exciting, choose a mixture of styles (some fast, some slow, some pop, and maybe even such old favorites as "The Hokey Pokey"). Stack your CDs next to your CD player so that they are easy to find during the party.

Dress for Dancing Success

When party time approaches, it's time to get dressed! Don your finest royal ball gown, shoes, and accessories. Do your hair and your fingernails. As the final touch, slip on your brand-new hair band—and get ready to feel the magic!